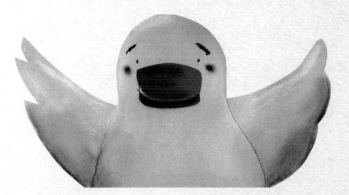

when I
GROW UP...

Written and Illustrated by
Paula Vásquez

GIBBS SMITH
TO ENRICH AND INSPIRE HUMANKIND

Teacher

Ester

wrote:

Who do you want to be like when you grow up?

When I grow up...

I want to have

antlers

so I can be as handsome as Dad.

—said Martin

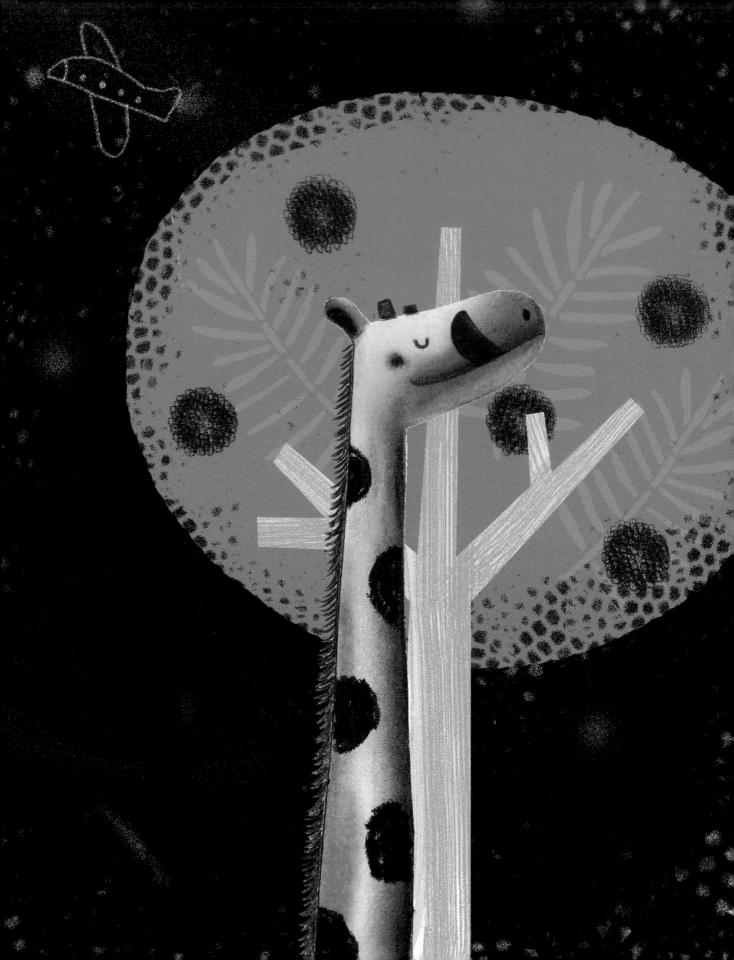

I want a
neck
like Mom's,
so I can reach the
juiciest apples.

—Julia said

I want

legs

like Dad's, so I can
run around the
meadow.

—Ema explained

I want a

tail

like Mom's, so I can

swing in the trees.

—shouted Ben

I want to be the king
of the jungle and have a
mane,
like my dad's.

—said Bert

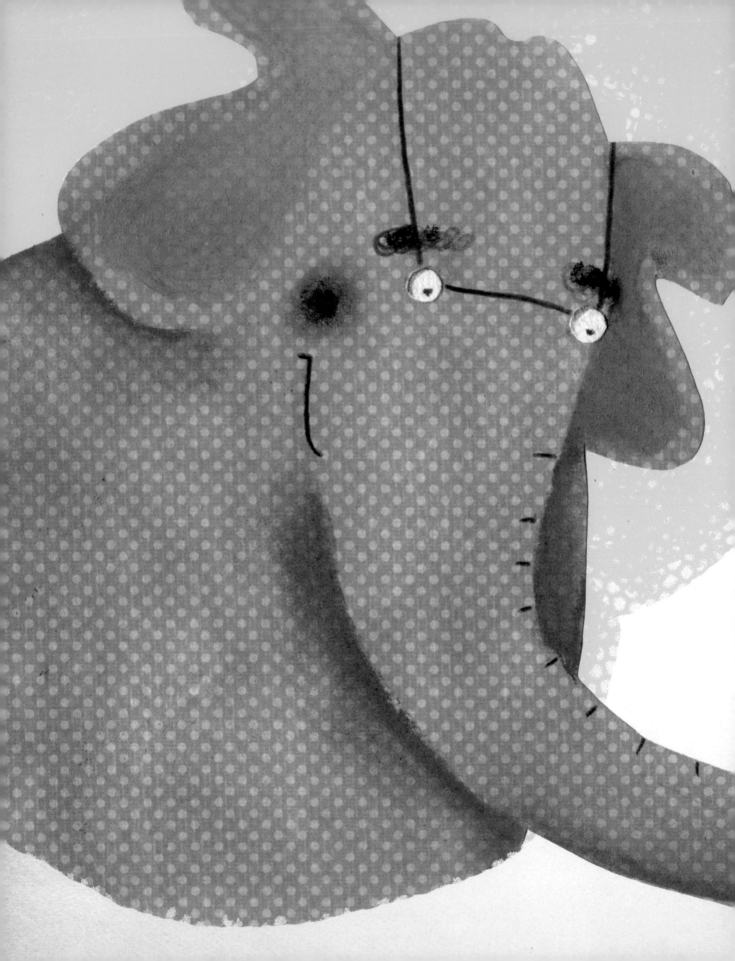

I would like to have a

trunk

like my grandpa's,
so I can cool down
on hot days.

—said Eric

And you, Johnny?

—Asked the teacher

Eeeem...
ummmm...
well...

I don't have

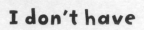

Mom's **tail,**

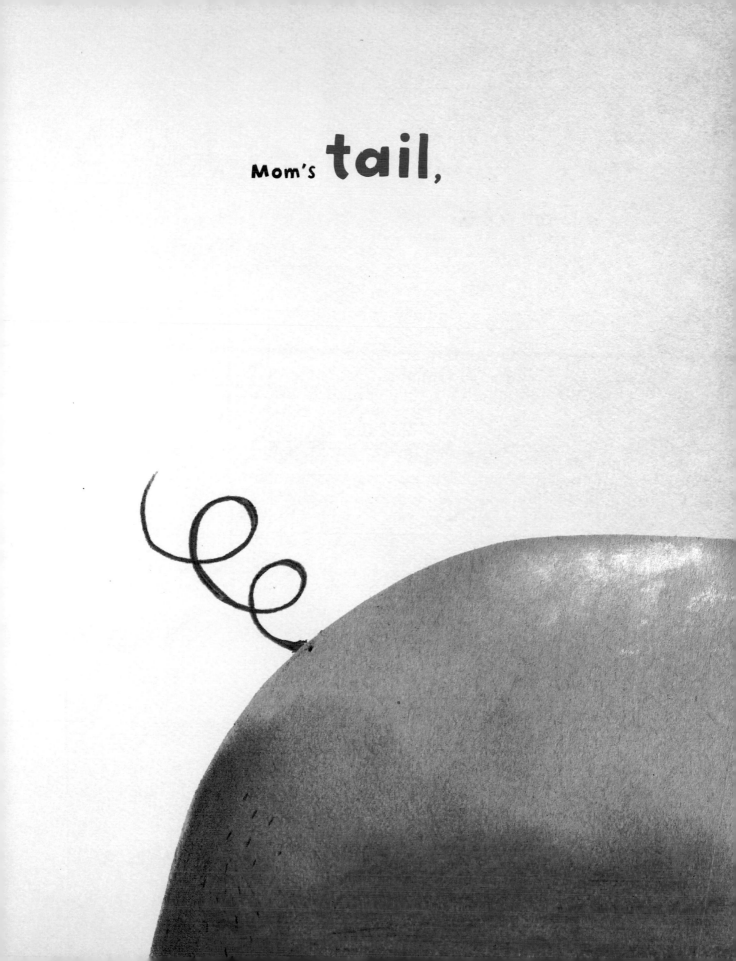

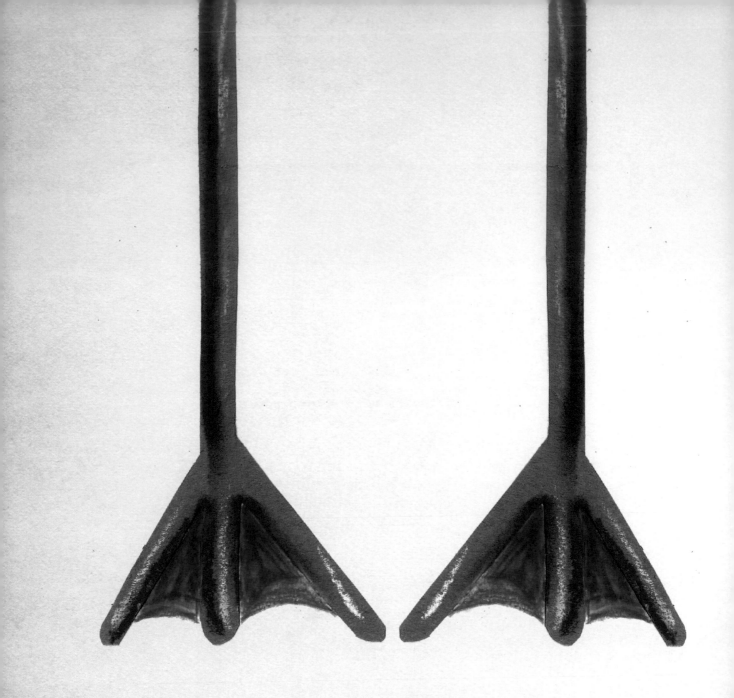

or Dad's

legs,

or Mom's

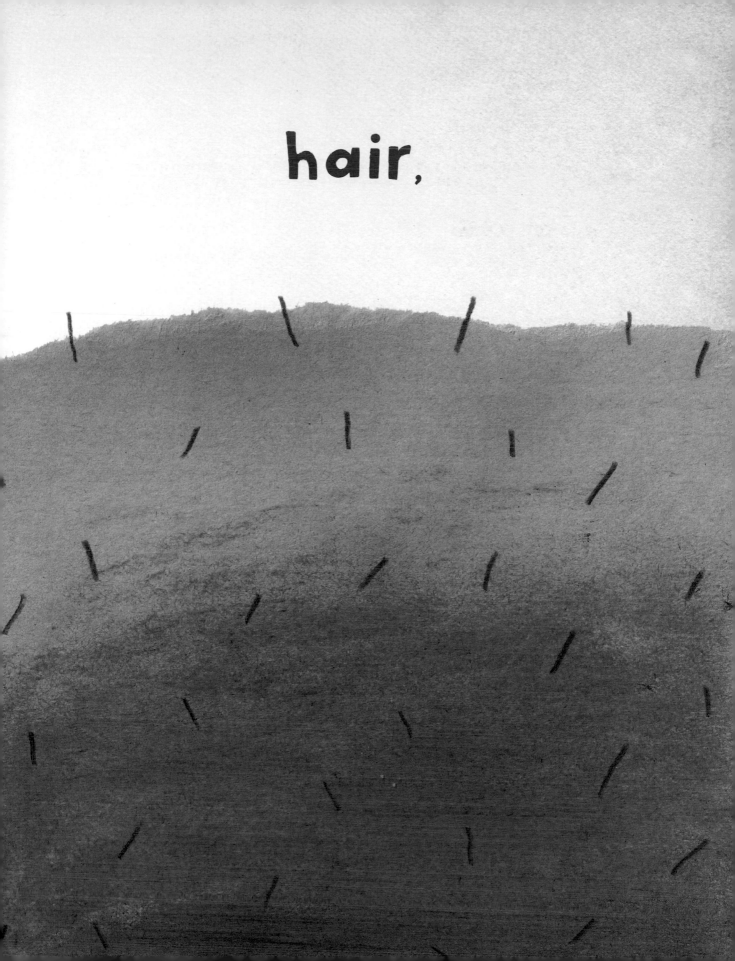

hair,

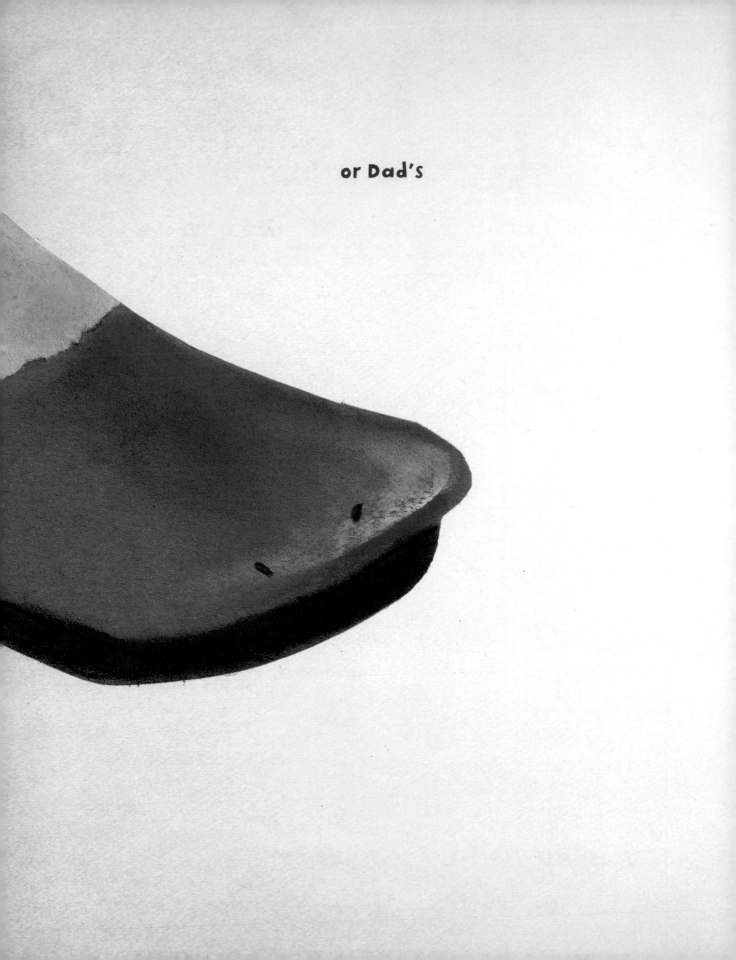

or Dad's

nose.

But...

When I grow up,

I want to **wallow in the mud** just like Mom,

be a **diving expert** like **Dad,**

sing in **Mom's band,**

and find delicious things

in the trash, just like Dad.

What great families you
all have!

—said Teacher Ester

Remember your homework
for tomorrow—draw a
picture of your family.

Paula Vásquez, an avowed artist from childhood, studied graphic design at the Universidad Católica de Chile, and honed her illustration skills with a post-graduate diploma from Finis Terrae University. She continued her studies at EINA Escola de Disseny i Art in Barcelona, Spain. She currently lives in Santiago de Chile writing and illustrating children's picture books.

Manufactured in Hong Kong in October 2016 by Toppan Printing, Co.

First Edition
21 20 19 18 17   5 4 3 2 1

Published by
Gibbs Smith
P.O. Box 667
Layton, Utah 84041

1.800.835.4993 orders
www.gibbs-smith.com

Designed by Paula Vásquez
Gibbs Smith books are printed on either recycled, 100% post-consumer waste, FSC-certified papers or on paper produced from sustainable PEFC-certified forest/controlled wood source. Learn more at www.pefc.org.

Library of Congress Control Number: 2016945726
ISBN: 978-1-4236-4689-1

Quack-Oink!

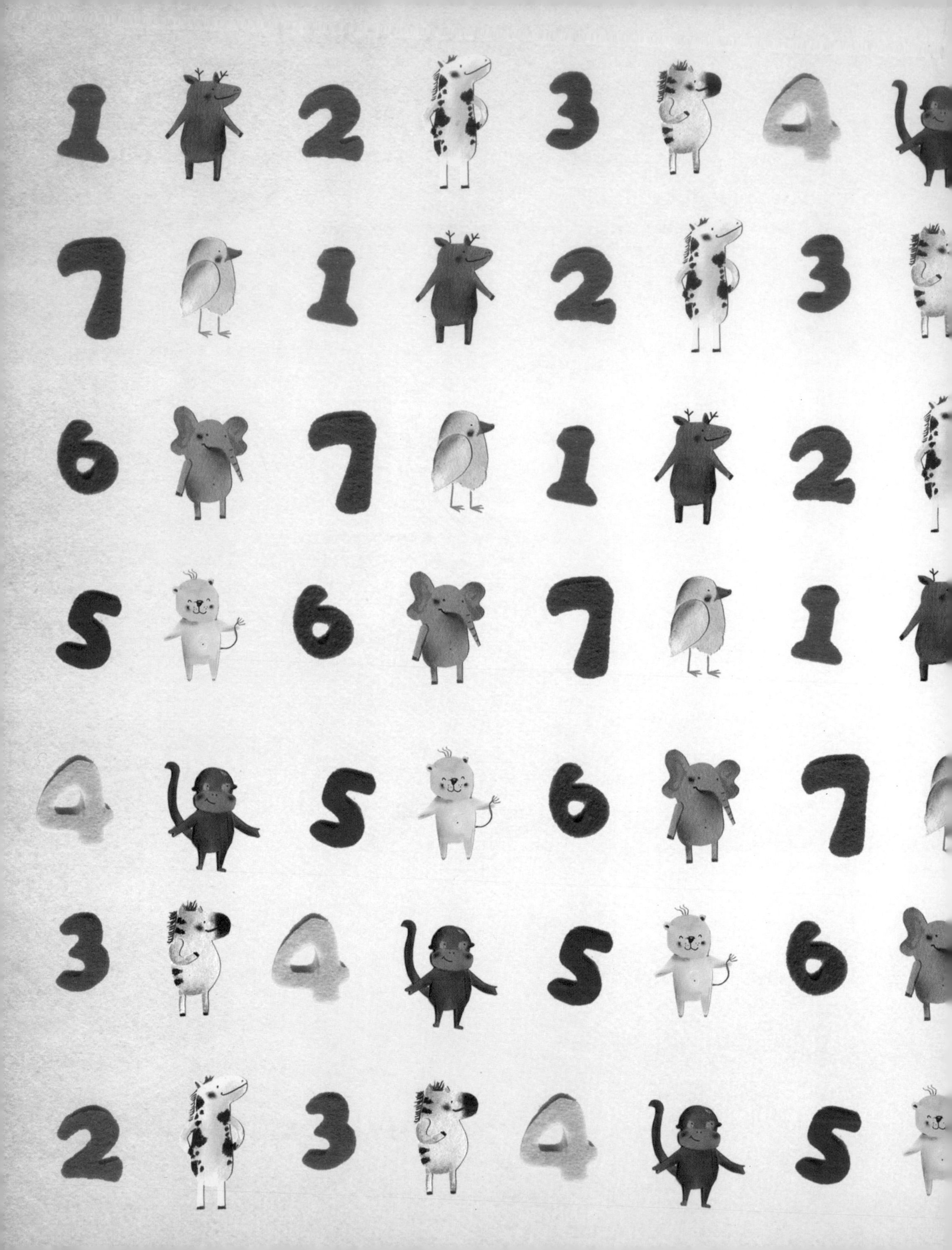